SOCCER SURPRISE

BY JAKE MADDOX

TEXT BY EMMA CARLSON BERNE

ILLUSTRATIONS BY KATIE WOOD

STONE ARCH BOOKS
a capstone imprint

Jake Maddox books are published by Stone Arch Books
A Capstone Imprint
1710 Roe Crest Drive
North Mankato, Minnesota 56003
www.capstonepub.com

Library of Congress Cataloging-in-Publication Data
Maddox, Jake.

Soccer surprise / by Jake Maddox ; text by Emma Carlson Berne ; illustrated by
Katie Wood.

p. cm. -- (Jake Maddox sports story)

Summary: Alex has just moved and joined a new soccer team, where she is
expected to play a different position; when her error leads to the team's first loss
she has to learn to put aside her pride and put the team first.

ISBN 978-1-4342-3291-5 (library binding)
ISBN 978-1-4342-3906-8 (pbk.)

1. Soccer teams--Juvenile fiction. 2. Soccer stories. 3. Disappointment--Juve-
nile fiction. 4. Pride and vanity--Juvenile fiction. [1. Soccer--Fiction. 2. Team-
work (Sports)--Fiction. 3. Pride and vanity--Fiction.] I. Berne, Emma Carlson. II.
Wood, Katie, ill. III. Title. IV. Series.

PZ7.M25643Som 2012
813.6--dc23

2011032225

Designer: Heather Kindseth
Production Specialist: Michelle Biedscheid

Printed in the United States of America in Stevens Point, Wisconsin.
072012
006847R

TABLE OF CONTENTS

CHAPTER ONE

A NEW POSITION

Tweeet! The referee's whistle rang out across the soccer field. It was the start of the second half against the Hornets.

After an uplifting halftime talk by Coach Mike, the Strikers were feeling good. They were only down by one goal.

As a midfielder, Alex had to be ready. Her eyes were on the ball in the center of the field. She was ready to boot it as soon as it came her way.

Alex had moved to Riverside last month. This was her first game with the Strikers. The team was undefeated so far. They only needed to win two more games and they'd go to regionals.

On her old team, Alex was a forward. She loved being a forward and was having a tough time being a midfielder.

Alex felt an unexpected pain in her throat at the thought of her old team, the Tiger Moths. She'd known most of those girls since kindergarten. Her two best friends, Mia and Stella, were the other two forwards.

Alex had cried for a week when her mom told her they were moving. She didn't need to start up again now in the middle of a game.

Alex knew she was better on offense. She just needed a chance to prove herself. Coach Mike would be sure to move her to forward once he saw her skills.

The score was 1-0. The Hornets were up. The Strikers needed to score in the next few minutes to tie the game. Then the game would go into overtime.

Alex looked around, catching the eye of Lin. Lin was a defender. Alex and Lin had become good friends in the last month.

"Come on, Strikers!" Alex shouted encouragingly. "Let's go, girls!"

Lin shouted, "Let's go, Strikers!"

The purple-shirted Hornets were quickly dribbling the ball down the field. They were easily moving around the Strikers' defense.

Alex could see the concentration on their faces. The Hornets' center midfielder looked right and left. Then she made a quick pass to one of the forwards. Lin was ready and stole the ball quickly.

"Alex!" Lin shouted.

Alex signaled that she was open. Lin passed her the ball. Alex gained control immediately. She dribbled down the field.

Alex passed the ball to Brooke, the Strikers' center midfielder. But in an instant, the Hornets' defense was on her.

"Here, Brooke!" yelled Nadia, one of the Strikers' forwards. She waved her arms. "I'm open!"

Brooke turned, saw Nadia, and passed her the ball. The black-and-white sphere shot across Alex's field of vision.

Without thinking, Alex fell back into the role of a forward. She intercepted the ball. In a quick one-two dribble, Alex ran toward the goal. The field seemed like a blur.

The net was wide open, the goalie running back into place. Alex booted the ball into the goal.

Smack! Nothing was as satisfying as that sound of her foot against the ball.

The ref's whistle blared. Then he shouted, "Offsides, penalty! Goal for Hornets!"

Alex looked around, confused. Then she saw the color of the goalie's jersey and the shocked faces of her teammates.

Alex realized that she hadn't saved the Strikers at all. In fact, she'd kicked the ball into the wrong goal.

As the Hornets celebrated their win, the Strikers sadly walked off the field.

"I guess you forgot which team you were playing for," Brooke said to Alex. Then she walked away.

CHAPTER TWO

A SIMPLE MISTAKE

Alex couldn't move. She felt frozen to the field. She was aware of the players leaving the field. Everyone was lining up for the post-game handshakes. She still couldn't believe what she had done!

Over by the bleachers, parents were packing up blankets and lawn chairs. It seemed like everything was in slow motion.

"Okay, team! Huddle up!" Coach Mike said.

Alex sank onto the grass beside the rest of the Strikers. The shock of what had just happened was beginning to wear off. She felt like she could think more clearly now. Scoring like that was an accident, of course.

She looked around at her teammates. They were all slumped on the grass. Alex swallowed. Everyone looked really bummed. Some girls even looked mad.

They can't be mad, Alex thought. *It was a mistake. It happens to everyone.*

"Okay, girls," Coach Mike began, hands on his hips. "This is our first loss of the season. It's a bummer."

"It's more than a bummer," Brooke said, shooting a mean look toward Alex. "Now we have to work extra hard to make playoffs."

"It wasn't our best game. But we had some really nice passing out there and some excellent aggressive play from the offense," Coach Mike said encouragingly. "You all gave it heart, and I'm proud of you."

He paused and glanced at Alex. Then he went on, "Now, some of you are still learning, and that's fine. Practice makes perfect."

"Whatever," Brooke said.

Alex just stared at the grass. He didn't mean her, did he? That didn't make sense. She wasn't still learning. She had been playing soccer since she was four! It was a simple mistake.

If I was still a forward, none of this would have happened, Alex thought.

Brooke got to her feet, her blond ponytail bobbing up and down. Beside her, Lin sat quietly, looking down at her lap.

"Coach, I think there is someone on this team who really messed up today," Brooke said, staring at Alex. "I think she should apologize."

Alex felt her face burn as everyone stared at her. Apologize? For a simple mistake? Brooke was crazy. But everyone else was nodding. Even Coach Mike seemed to be waiting for her to say something. The silence stretched out.

Finally, Alex took a deep breath. "Um, I know I kicked the ball into the wrong goal," she said. "But that was a total mistake. It could happen to anyone. I'm just used to being a forward."

Her words sounded a little more defensive than she'd intended. She looked around for support but instead saw only angry faces.

A wave of confusion swept over Alex. Obviously she hadn't meant to score for the other team. Couldn't anyone understand that? Alex looked around. Only Lin looked sympathetic.

Coach Mike spoke up. "All right, players, let's call it a day," he said. "It was a tough game, and I think we all need some rest. See you all at practice tomorrow."

Everyone started gathering their things and heading toward the parking lot. Alex took awhile finding her water bottle. When she got to her feet, she found she was alone on the sidelines.

She walked toward her mom's car and caught a glimpse of Lin, disappearing into her parents' car.

"Lin, wait up!" Alex called, running toward her.

Lin turned around. "Uh, sorry, Alex, got to go!" she called back. "Dentist appointment. See you tomorrow."

Alex slowed down, dragging her cleats through the gravel. She wasn't looking forward to the car ride home.

CHAPTER THREE

LONG DRIVE HOME

Alex climbed into the minivan and slammed the door. After buckling her seat belt, she slumped low in her seat. She propped her cleats on the dashboard as her mom pulled out of the parking lot.

"Now, hon —" Mom began right away. She glanced at her daughter and said, "Alex Hausman! I've told you a thousand times not to put your feet up there."

Alex sighed and thumped her feet to the floor. Her mom continued, "I know you're probably feeling bad about that goal, but everyone makes mistakes. I'm sure it's happened to some of the other girls before."

"Mom, that's not it!" Alex said, pushing herself up in the seat. "I told them all it was just a mistake, and everyone just stared at me."

"They were probably upset about losing their first game," Mom said. "Give them a little time." She glanced over at Alex. "But honey, you know you are defense. What were you doing trying to shoot anyway?"

Alex stared at her lap. "I forgot. I'm so used to being a forward. I just wanted to help out my new team," she mumbled, twisting her fingers. "Anyway, I should be offense. I was back home."

Mom steered the car into their driveway and turned off the engine. She sat for a moment, staring out through the windshield at their tidy brick house.

"Alex," she said softly. "I know this move has been hard on you, but this is home now. And everyone here is going to see what a great player you are. You need to prove yourself and gain their trust."

Alex picked at a loose thread on her shiny soccer shorts. "I feel dumb stuck at midfield," she mumbled. "No one here knows I used to be an awesome forward."

Mom patted her knee. "Maybe not," Mom said. "But that was in the past. Now you're a midfielder."

Alex stared straight ahead through the windshield.

"Alex, it doesn't matter what position you play. Just have fun," Mom said cheerfully. She got out of the car. "I made beef stew for tonight. Doesn't that make you feel a little better?" she asked.

"Yeah, thanks, Mom," Alex managed to reply.

But as she followed her mother into the house, she thought that the only thing that would make her feel better would be forgetting this day ever happened.

CHAPTER FOUR

BAD TO WORSE

The next afternoon, Alex walked onto the field with determination. The bright sunshine and light breeze tossing the treetops made her feel as if the incident yesterday had never happened. Mom was right. Everyone else had probably already forgotten about it too.

Most of the Strikers were already on the field, kicking balls from one to the other or stretching on the sidelines.

Duffel bags and soccer balls were scattered on the grass. Coach Mike was sitting on the bench looking at his clipboard.

Alex dumped her bag next to the others and hurried over to Lin and Brooke, who were passing a ball back and forth.

"Hi guys," she greeted them cheerfully.

"Hi," Lin said back, and passed the ball to Brooke. But Brooke just narrowed her eyes and looked away.

Alex's mouth fell open. Was Brooke actually still mad about yesterday? She looked back at Lin, who gave a little shrug.

Alex opened her mouth to say something to Lin, but before she could, Coach Mike called, "Okay, players, get into position for drills!"

Brooke was just being crabby, Alex decided as she took her place in one of the two double lines. She tried to catch the eye of Christie, her passing partner, but Christie just frowned and looked away.

Alex swept her eyes over the two lines of girls passing the ball back and forth. No one looked at her. In fact, it seemed like everyone was ignoring her. There was a definite tension in the air.

Alex booted the ball back to Christie as hard as she could. *They can't forgive one mistake?* she thought. *They are just stuck-up, that's all. The Tiger Moths never would have treated me like this.*

Alex's stomach churned uneasily as the practice dragged on. After drills they scrimmaged. Alex was not surprised when nobody would pass her the ball.

At the end of practice Coach gave a pep talk about the upcoming game.

"We lost a tough game yesterday," Coach Mike said. "But I know we're ready to win big tomorrow. I'll see you all here at four o'clock sharp. Everyone get a good night's sleep."

The girls broke up, huddling in little groups as they packed up their gear. Alex grabbed her bag and hurried over to the bench, where Lin was changing her cleats for a pair of sneakers.

"Hey, Lin!" Alex said. "Do you want to come over? My mom can drive you home later."

Lin seemed uncomfortable. A couple of girls nearby looked at Lin, waiting to hear her answer.

Lin finished tying her shoes and grabbed Alex's arm. She pulled her off to the side of the field. A couple of tall bushes provided a handy screen as Lin leaned in close.

"Listen, Alex, I have to talk to you," Lin whispered. She shifted a little. "Everyone's still kind of mad about yesterday."

"I cannot believe this!" Alex exclaimed, her voice rising. "One tiny mistake and I'm going to be blamed for the rest of the season!" She crossed her arms. "Look, I'm sorry it was the first loss, okay?"

"Calm down, Alex," Lin whispered, making patting motions with her hands. "It's not that it was the first loss, exactly."

"Then what's the problem?" Alex asked.

"It's just that, well, some of the girls feel like you should say you're sorry," Lin said. "Even if it was just a mistake. You are being kind of rude about the whole thing."

"If anyone is being rude, it's not me," Alex replied angrily. "And I suppose you think I should apologize, too?"

Alex didn't know why she was getting mad at Lin. Lin was just trying to help her. But she felt like she had to get mad at someone.

"Well . . ." Lin looked down and scuffed the gravel with her feet. "I guess, yeah. That is what I think. I think you should say you're sorry."

"Well, I don't," Alex snapped and stomped away.

CHAPTER FIVE

PULL IT TOGETHER

Her mom was standing over the stove when Alex snuck in the back door. She walked fast through the kitchen, hoping she could make it to the stairs before Mom saw her red eyes.

"Hey, Alex," Mom said behind her. "How was practice?"

"Fine," she said in what she hoped was a casual voice.

"What's wrong, honey?" Mom asked as she sat down on a high stool at the kitchen island. She patted the seat next to her.

Alex sighed and sat on the stool next to her mom. She propped her head on her arm.

"Mom, I just don't know what to do!" she said. "The team's totally mad at me. Lin says they all want me to say I'm sorry for scoring for the other team. And I want to, but I feel so stupid now because it's been too long. And they're all going to hate me forever, and I'll never have any friends here. This place is awful! This never would have happened back at home." A couple of tears spilled down her cheeks.

Her mom rubbed Alex's back, the way she used to when Alex was little.

"The girls can't stay mad forever. Your next game is tomorrow, right?" her mom asked.

Alex nodded.

"Just make sure you're the best team player out there," Mom said. "Don't move one step outside of your position, pass to everyone, play hard, and play fair. That's what made you such a good teammate on the Tiger Moths, and that's what will make you one on the Strikers."

She returned to stirring the sauce and said, "I wish I could be there tomorrow, but I have a work meeting. But I'll be thinking of you. You can do it, Alex."

"Thanks, Mom," Alex replied. "I'll do my best."

Alex trailed out of the kitchen. She was exhausted. Back in her room, she dropped her duffel bag on her bed and stared in the mirror over her dresser. She had puffy eyes and messy hair. She looked terrible.

"I need to pull it together. Play hard, play fair," she said to herself out loud. "I can do this."

CHAPTER SIX

THE PASSING PROBLEM

"Okay, Strikers, look alive!" Coach Mike called from the sidelines the next afternoon. He stood with his hands on his hips. He hoped his team was ready.

Out on the field, the Strikers were ready for the kickoff against the Thunder. Brooke was facing off against a tall girl with braces and a brown ponytail.

Back in her new position, Alex crossed her fingers and took a deep breath.

No one had talked to her as they'd arrived for the game, but her mom was right. She wasn't a Tiger Moth anymore. She was a Striker now, and she had to adjust. Alex needed to be a better team player.

Tweeeet! The ref's whistle sounded. Brooke and the Thunder's center fought for the ball. Brooke gained control. The parents on the sidelines cheered loudly as she swiftly dribbled toward the goal.

A Thunder defender was on her, but she passed to the left. Nadia captured the ball, ducking around a Thunder defender, and shot at the goal.

The Thunder's goalie slid left and caught the ball with her arms outstretched over her head.

The players fought for position as the Thunder's goalie threw the ball toward the tall center. The center easily blocked the ball, whipping around and dribbling fast down the field. The Thunder's coach yelled and jumped up and down on the sidelines.

The girl came closer, and Alex tensed for action. Christie ran up to the girl and stole the ball. Alex saw her looking around for someone to pass to. This was her chance!

"Here, Christie!" she yelled, jumping up and waving her arms. But Christie glanced over and looked away fast. She passed instead to Brooke, even though she had two Thunder defenders guarding her.

Why didn't Christie pass to me? Alex wondered. She was way closer and more open than Brooke.

But Alex didn't have time to think about the situation for very long. The Striker center had regained control of the ball again and was dribbling toward her, fast.

Alex swooped in front of the girl, neatly stealing the ball. Then, as carefully as she could, dribbled forward and shot to Nadia. There. She breathed a tiny sigh of relief.

The whole team had seen her stay in position and shoot to the offense, just like she was supposed to.

But her teammates must not have noticed. Just before halftime, another forward, Marissa, had the ball on a corner kick. Alex positioned herself for the ball, but Marissa looked at her and looked away. She shot straight to Christie, who dribbled it up to Nadia.

Alex was sad and confused. She went through the motions of playing the game, but her mind was whirling.

Was her team ignoring her? How was she going to prove that she was a team player if they wouldn't pass to her? Alex could feel sweat collecting on her forehead, and not just because of the heat of the day.

Tweeet! The ref blew his whistle. "That's the half!" he shouted.

Alex headed for the sidelines with relief. Maybe everything would get cleared up during the break.

CHAPTER SEVEN

THE SILENT TREATMENT

"Okay, team. Nice work so far," Coach Mike said, gathering the team into a huddle. "The defense is a little odd."

Alex saw him glance at her with a puzzled look, but she looked away. The coach went on, "But we're playing strong. Keep it up!"

"Strikers!" the players yelled as they broke huddle. They scattered to grab their water bottles before the break ended.

Alex looked around for Lin, only to see her friend disappearing into the bathroom. The rest of the players were gathered in little groups, chatting and resting.

No one was talking to Alex. Finally, she couldn't stand the awkwardness one more second.

"Hey, that center is big, huh?" she said to Christie, trying to sound casual.

Christie looked up from relacing her cleats, saw that Alex was speaking to her, then very pointedly looked away without answering.

Alex's face turned bright red. She looked over at Brooke, who was standing nearby, but Brooke looked away also. Alex got the hint. They were all giving her the silent treatment.

She was still being punished for her one little mistake. That's why no one would pass to her. And not even Lin was here to help her out.

Alex felt helpless. Everyone was staring at her with mean looks. Only Coach Mike was oblivious, talking with some parent over by the bleachers.

Alex thought she'd never felt so alone. Just then, she saw Lin coming back over to the sidelines. She smiled hopefully at her friend. But Lin looked away, too.

Alex couldn't take it anymore. She felt her throat swell and tears spill from her eyes, pouring down her cheeks. She spun on her heel and ran away.

CHAPTER EIGHT

SLURPEE SURPRISE

Alex ran past the parking lot and through the quiet streets. She was sobbing so hard, she could hardly see. The houses on either side flashed by in a watery blur. Her cleats clacked on the sidewalk.

Finally, her sobs slowed and she stopped near a low wall in a yard. She laid her head down on her knees. Her mom had been wrong. Playing hard and playing fair wasn't enough — at least not for her.

Alex got up and wandered down the sidewalk. She didn't have anywhere to go. She couldn't go back to the game, not after running off the field like that. And she couldn't go home until the game was supposed to be over.

She dragged her feet along the sidewalk until she came to the corner, where a small convenience store stood. After her horrible day, she decided she could use a treat.

In the reflection of the glass window, she saw a figure approach. Alex swung around. Coach Mike was standing there, his hands in his jacket pockets, smiling.

Alex stepped backward in surprise. She didn't know what to say. "Coach! What are you doing here?" she spluttered.

"Thirsty?" Coach Mike said in response.

He didn't act like there was anything unusual about a coach leaving his team in the middle of a game.

"Uh . . ." Alex stammered.

But the coach already had his hand on the metal push bar of the door. "Wait here," he instructed, pointing to a green bench nearby.

Alex sank down on the bench. When she looked up a minute later, Coach Mike was standing in front of her, holding two giant cherry Slurpees.

"So," he said, handing her a Slurpee and sitting down beside her on the bench. "What's the trouble?"

"Uh, Coach? Who's coaching the game?" Alex asked.

Her Slurpee was freezing her hands, so she took a drink and set it down beside her.

"Oh, that!" Coach Mike said. He waved his hand. "I handed the reins to Brooke's father for a few minutes. He's been trying to get my job all season anyway." He eyed Alex over the clear plastic Slurpee top. "All joking aside, Alex, I can see you're having trouble with the team."

"Is it that obvious?" Alex joked weakly. She felt a wave of shame rise up in her throat. It was bad enough that the other players hated her. But to have the coach know about it somehow seemed worse.

Coach Mike nodded. "You think I spend all of my time staring at that clipboard?" he asked. "Alex, I bet it wasn't easy, moving here in the middle of the school year and leaving your friends behind."

Alex nodded, the familiar lump rising in her throat again.

Coach Mike continued, "It may be selfish of me, but I was glad you joined the Strikers, even if you did have to leave your old team. You're a great midfielder. Tall, strong, and quick."

He held up his hand as Alex's mouth opened to respond. "I know you played offense on your old team," he said, "and I'm sure you were great as a forward. But I don't think that was the right spot for you." He looked right at Alex. "I need you at defense."

Alex nodded. Her old coach had never told her she was needed before. It was nice, feeling needed. "But Coach," she said. "I don't know how I can play if everyone hates me."

Coach Mike stood up and flipped his cup into a trash can with one decisive gesture. "Nobody hates you, Alex," he said, smiling at her. "They just don't know you. There's only one way to make this whole thing better, and I think you know what you need to do."

Alex looked up. "Isn't it a little too late to apologize to the team?" she asked hesitantly, almost hoping there would be a different answer.

Coach Mike shook his head and looked at his watch. "It's never too late," he said. "I know you didn't mean to score for the other team. Mistakes happen. But it would really make everyone feel better if you just said those two magic words."

"I know, I know," Alex said.

"Come on. Game's almost over. Now's the perfect time," he said, turning and jogging back in the direction of the field.

Alex watched until he was about half a block away, then rose slowly and followed. He was right. It was now or never.

CHAPTER NINE

HARD TO SAY

Alex walked slowly back up the street, through the parking lot, and to the edge of the field. From where she was standing, she could see that the game must have just ended. The Strikers were scattered on the sidelines, taking off their cleats and talking.

Alex stood still, twisting her fingers. The last thing in the world she wanted to do was apologize, but Coach Mike was already waving her over.

There's no way out, she told herself. *You have to do it.*

Alex felt her legs move across the soft turf as if they were moving on their own. One by one, her teammates turned to face her, their eyes curious. She saw Lin standing over to the side. Was it just Alex's imagination, or did Lin look hopeful?

The talking died down and the players fell silent. Coach Mike stepped up next to Alex and laid a hand on her shoulder.

"Listen up, please," he said. "Alex would like to tell all of us something. I'd like you all to listen to her with respect." He gave Alex's shoulder a firm pat and stepped back.

Alex stood alone in front of the sea of watching eyes. Her stomach was churning.

Please, please don't let me throw up, she prayed silently.

Then she caught Lin's sympathetic face, and her friend gave her an encouraging nod.

Alex's stomach steadied itself. She opened her mouth and somehow, the words started coming out.

"Um," she started. "I just wanted to say that . . . I know you all are really mad at me. I'm sorry for scoring that wrong goal the other day."

She looked at their faces. Brooke and Christie looked suspicious. Alex knew she needed to say more. She shifted her weight.

Her palms were clammy, and she could feel a trickle of sweat running down the side of her face.

"I'm new here," Alex went on, "and everyone already knew each other. I just wanted to help the team. Maybe I was trying too hard. I'm sorry about that. I didn't want to be a ball hog or mess everything up." The words seemed to be getting easier now. At the back, near the bleachers, she could see Coach Mike, smiling and nodding encouragingly.

"But most of all," Alex went on. "I'm sorry I didn't say sorry earlier." She paused. "Does that make sense?"

A couple of the girls, including Brooke, nodded.

"I don't know why I didn't," Alex added, "except that sorry is hard to say. I know I haven't started out great, but I'm going to try to do better." She stopped talking. No one moved.

The only sounds were distant traffic and a bird singing in a nearby tree. Alex's heart sank. Was this all a mistake? Did they all still hate her?

Then from the back of the group, came the sound of clapping. Alex craned her neck.

Lin and Coach Mike were both applauding, big smiles on their faces. Then the applause spread through the rest of the group.

Brooke, Nadia, and Christie were all smiling. And Alex couldn't help smiling back.

"Thanks, guys," she whispered. She didn't think anyone heard her, but Lin pushed her way through the crowd and grabbed Alex up in a hug.

"We're happy to have you on our team," said Brooke.

"Really?" Alex asked.

"Really," Brooke said. "Now, enough talking, let's celebrate our latest win!"

ABOUT THE AUTHOR

Emma Carlson Berne has written more than a dozen books for children and young adults, including teen romance novels, biographies, and history books. She lives in Cincinnati, Ohio, with her husband, Aaron, her son, Henry, and her dog, Holly.

ABOUT THE ILLUSTRATOR

Katie Wood fell in love with drawing when she was very small. Since graduating from Loughborough University School of Art and Design in 2004, she has been living her dream working as a freelance illustrator. From her studio in Leicester, England, she creates bright and lively illustrations for books and magazines all over the world.

GLOSSARY

CENTER (SEN-tur) — one of the players whose job is to score points

DEFENDER (de-FEN-dur) — a person playing defense, trying to keep the other team from scoring

DEFENSE (DI-fens) — the team or players that are trying to prevent the other side from scoring

FORWARD (FOR-wurd) — part of the offense; responsible for most of the scoring

GOALIE (GOH-lee) — the person who guards the goal and prevents the other team from scoring

INTERCEPTED (in-tur-SEPT-id) — stole the ball

MIDFIELDER (MID-feel-dur) — part of the defense; they help with ball control and passing

OFFENSE (AW-fenss) — the team that is attacking or trying to score, or the players whose job it is to score

OFFSIDES (OFF-sidez) — a penalty when a player has moved ahead of the ball

PENALTY (PEN-uhl-tee) — a punishment that a team suffers for breaking the rules

SCRIMMAGED (SKRIM-ijd) — played a game for practice, usually between members of the same team

DISCUSSION QUESTIONS

1. After Alex scored a point for the other team, the other girls were mad. However, they weren't mad about the goal. They were mad that Alex didn't apologize for her mistake. Do you think they had a right to be mad? Why or why not?

2. Were you surprised that Coach Mike left the game to help Alex? If you were the coach, would you have done the same thing? Explain your answer.

3. Why do you think it was so hard for Alex to apologize to her teammates?

WRITING PROMPTS

1. After the big loss, Coach Mike gave the team a little pep talk. Write your own pep talk to make the Strikers feel better.

2. Would you rather be a defensive player or an offensive player? Write a paragraph explaining your answer.

3. How do you think the Strikers ended the season? Did they lose in the first round of playoffs? Did they win state? Write a small article for the school newspaper about the Strikers' season.

SOCCER FUN

In the United States, the sport is called SOCCER. Nearly everywhere else in the world, fans call it FOOTBALL. Soccer is the world's most popular sport.

A **NEW BALL** is designed for every World Cup, which takes place every four years. Billions of people around the world watch the World Cup.

The Romans played a game called **HARPASTUM**. This is said to be the beginning of soccer in the modern era. However, the origins of soccer can be traced back more than 2,000 years to China.

MIA HAMM holds the record for most world game goals by a male or female player. She has **158** goals in world games in her career.

CRISTIANO RONALDO is one of the most famous and highest-paid soccer players in the world. He makes over $17 MILLION a year.

BRAZIL has won five World Cups, which is the most in the world (1958, 1962, 1970, 1994, and 2002).

KRISTINE LILLY of the United States has played in more soccer games than any other man or woman in the world. She played in 352 matches before she retired.

GIRLS
with
GAME

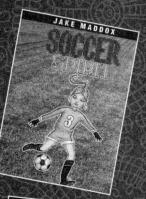

When Alex and her family move to a new town, she doesn't just leave behind old friends. She leaves behind her old soccer team as well. To make matters worse, Alex learns she'll have to play a different position on her new team. Can Alex adjust to her new life both on and off the field? Or will she be stuck on the bench?

JAKE MADDOX

Power, Pride, Skill, and Spirit.
Sports stories for every athlete.

MORE FROM JAKE MADDOX

008-011 RL: 2.9 GRL: M

Illustrations by Katie Wood

▾▾ STONE ARCH BOOKS™
a capstone imprint www.capstonepub.com